T0407065

Understanding Identity

Anti-Bias Learning: Social Justice in Action

By Emily Chiariello

21st Century
Junior Library

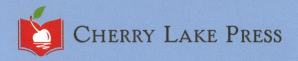

Published in the United States of America by Cherry Lake Publishing Group
Ann Arbor, Michigan
www.cherrylakepublishing.com

Developed with help from Learning for Justice, a project of the Southern Poverty Law Center. With special
thanks to Monita Bell and Hoyt Phillips.
Reading Adviser: Beth Walker Gambro, MS, Ed., Reading Consultant, Yorkville, IL

Photo Credits: © Monkey Business Images/Shutterstock.com, cover, 1; © pixelheadphoto digitalskillet/
Shutterstock.com, 4; © wavebreakmedia/Shutterstock.com, 6; © Elzbieta Sekowska/Shutterstock.com, 8;
© Tippman98x/Shutterstock.com, 10; © P Maxwell Photography/Shutterstock.com, 12; © Juan Ci/
Shutterstock.com, 14; © Rido/Shutterstock.com, 16; © hanapon1002/Shutterstock.com, 18;
© ESB Professional/Shutterstock.com, 20

Library of Congress Cataloging-in-Publication Data has been filed and is available at catalog.loc.gov

Cherry Lake Publishing Group would like to acknowledge the work of the Partnership for 21st Century Learning,
a Network of Battelle for Kids. Please visit http://www.battelleforkids.org/networks/p21 for more information.

Printed in the United States of America
Corporate Graphics

CONTENTS

5 Me!

9 History and Culture

13 All My Layers

17 Pride

19 Always Me

22 Glossary

23 Find Out More

24 Index

24 About the Author

What parts of your identity do you share with members of your family? What about friends or classmates?

Me!

I like me.

Who are you? Do you like who you are? Can you talk about yourself and your family? Can you talk about your **identity**?

Identity is all of the wonderful things that make you YOU.

Identity describes the **characteristics**, traits, and qualities you **possess** as an individual human being. Your personal identity makes you unique!

Think about some of the things that make you and your friends different. What makes you similar?

Some identities are your gender, race, interests, abilities, language, family income, appearance, age, size, and religion.

Identity also connects you to other people who share the same characteristics, traits, and qualities. You and those people are part of the same **identity group**. You have some experiences in common.

For example, Aisha is a tall Muslim girl with brown skin who plays basketball and speaks English. She shares an identity with other Muslims, other girls, other brown-skinned people, other basketball players, and other English speakers.

Think!

What are you most proud of about yourself?

Your grandparents' grandparents were already writing *your* story.

History and Culture

I know where I come from.

Do you know your family's history? What about your culture? What are some of the important things people should know about your family? What have people who share your identities achieved or contributed to the world?

The story of you started a long time ago. **Generations** of family and community have had experiences—both good and bad. These experiences have paved the way for you to be who you are today.

Juneteenth started in Texas, but the day is now celebrated all over the country.

That history is a part of your identity. Knowing where you come from helps you understand your identity.

But history is only one part of your identity. For instance, take Joshua. His dad is African American. His family has lived in Alabama for generations. Joshua's dad knows his **ancestors** were from Africa, but many important details about his family history are unknown. This is one of the harms caused by slavery. Every year, they gather together for Juneteenth—a holiday that celebrates the freedom of enslaved Africans living in the United States.

Ask Questions!

Where did your name come from? What does it mean? Talk to your parents or caregivers to find out the history of your name.

See if you can name all your delicious layers!

All My Layers

I am many things.

Once you start thinking about your identity, you will realize that you are made of many beautiful layers. Each one of those layers is an identity. Your identities are the ingredients that make you special. You are a mixture of all those ingredients!

Think of a delicious peanut butter and jelly sandwich. It wouldn't be as delicious without the PB *and* the J!

When you think and talk about who you are, do you include all of your identities? Or do you include just one or some of them?

Lena reads with her daughter in American Sign Language (ASL).

That PB&J sandwich is so yummy not just because of the peanut butter or the jelly. It's delicious because the two flavors mix together to make a new one. The same is true for you. Without all the parts of your identity, you wouldn't be fully YOU!

The way our identities combine or **intersect** is an important part of who we are. This is true both for you and for other people.

Meet Lena. Lena is a mom and a doctor. She is also Deaf. She is all of these things at the same time. This combination shines through in her unique gifts and experiences.

You can feel proud of yourself and the things you have done,
like when you do well on a test. You can feel proud of your family
or school or community too.

Pride

I am proud of who I am.

Have you noticed how many feelings you have? There are a lot. You can feel shy or happy or scared or silly, sometimes all in the same day!

Pride is another feeling. It means that you feel good about who you are. A healthy feeling of pride comes when we **value** our identity without making anyone else feel bad about theirs.

For example, Keith loves his family's **tradition** of going to church on Sundays. But he also knows there is nothing wrong with his friends who do not go to church.

You might act differently when you're at swim practice than when you're at band practice, but you're always you.

Always Me

I stay true to me.

In one day, you might find yourself at home, at school, on the bus, in the library, or in the grocery store. Each **environment** is different.

Sometimes, you change your behavior in new environments, like being quiet in a library or taking off your shoes in someone's home. But even when you change your behavior, your identity stays the same.

Sebastian knows he's the same person—whether he's talking with his *abuela* or scoring a goal on the soccer field.

Sebastian is an athlete and very smart. He can speak *two* languages! When he is on the field, he is loud and speaks in English. But when he is at home, he speaks to his **abuela** softly in Spanish.

Growing up means finding ways to be true to you, no matter where you go!

Create!

Write an acrostic poem using your first name and words that describe you. Begin each line of your poem with a letter from your name.

GLOSSARY

abuela (uhb-WAY-luh) the Spanish word for *grandmother*

ancestors (AN-sess-tuhrz) members of your family who lived a long time ago

characteristics (kehr-ik-tuh-RIH-stiks) qualities or features

environment (in-VYE-ruhn-muhnt) the circumstances, objects, or conditions that surround you

generations (jeh-nuh-RAY-shuhnz) people who are born around the same time

identity (eye-DEN-tuh-tee) who you are

identity group (eye-DEN-tuh-tee GROOP) people who share the same characteristics, qualities, and experiences

intersect (in-tuhr-SEKT) to meet or cross something

possess (puh-ZESS) to have or own

tradition (truh-DIH-shuhn) a custom, idea, or belief handed down from one generation to another

value (VAL-yoo) to believe something is important

FIND OUT MORE

WEBSITES

Learning for Justice Classroom Resources—Students texts, tasks, and more
https://www.learningforjustice.org/classroom-resources

Learning for Justice—Learn more about anti-bias work and find the full Social Justice Standards framework
https://www.learningforjustice.org

Social Justice Books—Booklists and a guide for selecting anti-bias children's books
https://socialjusticebooks.org

Welcoming Schools—Creating safe and welcoming schools
https://www.welcomingschools.org

INDEX

A
abilities, 7
age, 7
appearance, 7

B
behavior, 19

C
characteristics, 5
community, 9
connections, 7
culture, 8–11

D
differences, 6

E
environments, 19
experiences, 7, 9, 15

F
family, 4, 9
feelings, 17
friends, 6

G
gender, 7
generations, family, 9
grandparents, 8
growing up, 21

H
history, 8–11

I
identity, 4–7
    as series of layers,
        13, 15
    staying true to, 18–21
    types of, 7
    valuing, 17
    what it is, 5
identity group, 7
income, family, 7
individuality, 5
interests, 7

L
language, 7
layers, personal, 12–15

M
"me"
    staying true to, 18–21

P
pride, 16–17

Q
qualities, 5

R
race, 7
religion, 7

S
similarities, 6
size, 7

T
traditions, 17
traits, 5

U
uniqueness, 5, 15

ABOUT THE AUTHOR

Emily Chiariello is an anti-bias educator, educational consultant, and former classroom teacher. She is the principal author of the Learning for Justice Social Justice Standards. Emily lives in Buffalo, New York.